CARTOON

CLIP-ART FOR YOUTH LEADERS 2

by Ron Wheeler

BAKER BOOK HOUSE
Grand Rapids, Michigan

Copyright 1991 by
Baker Book House Company

ISBN: 0-8010-9714-2

Second printing, July 1992

Printed in the United States of America

I dedicate this book to Jesus.
May he honor the efforts
of those who created this book
by using it to glorify his name
and to further his kingdom.

Acknowledgments

I received lots of help in the production of this book. I am grateful to the staff of Baker Book House for their editing, production, and marketing expertise. Brian Reckling was a big help in getting me started on this project by categorizing file after file of cartoons. My secretary, Felicia Surber, helped in freeing up my time to work on this book. My wife, Cindy, has been a big help with her support and encouragement. And our two kids, Audrey and Byron, occupied themselves with activities so I could spend extra time on this project. With all of this help and with your use of the book, this project has truly been a team approach by many people with one desired goal in mind . . . the glorification of God and the furtherance of his kingdom.

Contents

Introduction

Welcome to *Cartoon Clip-Art for Youth Leaders 2.* You will find it similar to the first book. It has virtually the same format; the chapter categories, tabs, and index help youth ministers find their appropriate clip-art. And the generic words and lettering give them the flexibility they want for customizing their messages. We found that youth leaders also want to use many of the old standard cartoon messages, just redrawn in fresh new ways. So we have provided that.

As you look more closely at the book you will find some differences. There are new cartoon ideas. In addition, several chapters were expanded to give more variety to your clip-art. "Music News," "Trip Info," and "Food Events" all nearly doubled in size. Since many youth ministers like using boxes and balloons to dress up their messages, we expanded the chapter "Borders, Symbols, and Letters." We now have some full-page decorative cartoon borders. We have added to "Spirit-Filled Fillers" cartoons containing message-oriented humor. There are several gag cartoons, comic strips, and cartoon pages that you can use to entertain as well as edify your audience. We now have close to 500 spot cartoons in the last chapter, compared to about 400 in the first book.

One complaint we had about our first book was that with cartoons on both sides of the page, those without copiers have to ruin some good cartoons to get the ones they want. We printed them that way to give you more cartoons to choose from at a cheaper price. The simple solution to that problem is to buy two clip-art books and use one for the right hand pages and the other for the left.

Another concern was whether we had enough of a racial mix. We have tried to address that in this book by having more minorities represented in the cartoons. One concern is that we do not want to communicate broad sweeping generalizations toward any ethnic group when we poke fun at a cartoon character.

HOW TO USE CLIP-ART

This clip-art book contains hundreds of cartoons that will enhance the effectiveness of youth leaders. Use them to illustrate

newsletters	postcards
posters	overhead transparencies
bulletins	fliers
T-shirts	greeting cards
tickets	newspaper ads
brochures	letterheads
programs	handouts
book covers	stickers
mailers	buttons
balloons	bulletin boards

Clearly there are nearly as many places to use clip-art as there are cartoon selections in this book. Let your imagination run wild.

So how do you use clip-art? Here are a few helpful hints:

1. *Do not clip the art you plan to use directly from this book.* Most youth ministers have access to a photocopy machine that makes clear enlargement or reduction copies (or a "fast-print" shop can do this). Clip from the copy, not the book. If a copier is not accessible, however, and you are stuck having to clip the pages, buy two books. Use one book to clip the right pages and the other to clip the left. That way you won't have to worry about losing the artwork on the back side of the page you are clipping.
2. When searching for the most appropriate clip-art, take advantage of the format of this book. If you need something to draw attention to an item in your newsletter, check the "Attention-Gettin' Headers." If you need something to fill a blank space, try "Spirit-Filled Fillers." If you are looking for an idea for a party, you may find it in "Party Promos" or "Food Events." An index has been provided to facilitate your search.
3. When you clip out the cartoon, allow a little white space around it.
4. Be creative in the use of this clip-art. Feel free to cut apart or combine clip-art from different sections to create the effect you want. For example, if your group has an annual hayride and you want to promote it as a really big event, make a customized T-shirt or poster design. Start with the

hayride logo in "Attention-Gettin' Headers," spell out the location of the event from the letters in "Borders, Symbols, and Letters," and add the date of the event from "Calendar Fixin's." You can promote the event by reducing the whole design and dropping it into your newsletter under the heading "Check It Out" from "Attention-Gettin' Headers."

5. Sketch out where you want the clip-art and the other elements before gluing them down. That way you will make sure everything fits and looks right.

6. Scotch tape or glue (using rubber cement) your elements onto stiff white board or light blue graph board. The graph board will help you keep your lines straight, yet won't show up when reproduced.

7. Be sure to eliminate any stray marks or pencil lines that may show up when reproduced.

That should cover it. Have fun!

ATTENTION-GETTIN' HEADERS

Do you want to draw special attention to a specific item in your newsletter? Have you had difficulty getting people to sign up or pay when they are supposed to? Or do you simply want to make sure your pearls of wisdom don't fall on deaf ears? This chapter will help you make sure your message is read. Also included are various coupons and tickets that can easily be customized.

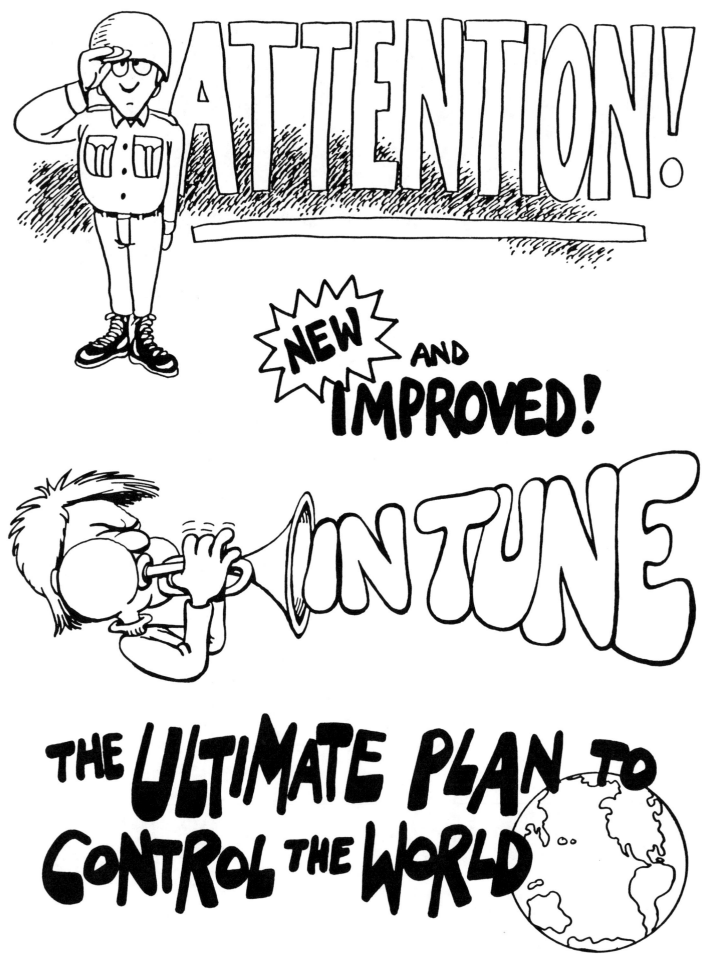

13

CONGRATULATIONS

COUPONS

TICKET FOR FUN!

ABSOLUTELY FREE

FREE PASS

2 FOR 1
BRING A FRIEND

COUPON FOR REDEMPTION

14

16

RESPOND TODAY!!

I'LL GO!

SHHHHHHHHH! IT'S A SECRET!

IT'S HERE!

WOW!!

FLASH

WELCOME

DON'T LOSE OUT!

A BRIGHT IDEA!

AMAZING

GRACE

R.S.V.P.

RESPOND SOON! VERY PROMPTLY!

Check it Out

JUST A REMINDER!

OOPS! I ALMOST FORGOT!

PARTY PROMOS

Need an idea for a party? How about "Video Impossible," a scavenger hunt with camcorders. Send everyone out to film such things as a fire fighter tap dancing, or any number of potentially embarrassing events. First team back wins. Then have fun watching each team's videos. Perhaps you already have a party theme in mind. If it isn't included in this chapter, check another chapter such as "Food Events" or "Calendar Fixin's" (holiday parties) for ideas. There are also some generic party heads so your big event can easily be promoted.

The Event of the Year!

HAY RIDE

SQUARE DANCE

BATTLE ZONE PARTY

AMAZING FEETS PARTY

AT THE HOP

MINIATURE GOLF

FILM NIGHT

28

SPORTS HEADS

Ready to play mix and match? These heads can be used in a variety of ways: to promote an event, to announce practice, or to recruit players. All the lettering styles are compatible so you can choose an opening, add the sport, and drop in the ending. For example, you can say "Come to a Volleyball Tournament," or "Hey, Soccer Fans," or "Come to a Football Game," or "It's Crazee Olympics Time," or simply "It's Time for Racketball."

COME TO A VOLLEYBALL TOURNAMENT

OKAY, I'M READY.

IT'S TIME FOR RACKETBALL

COME TO A   HEY

LET'S GO TO A   IT'S

LET'S PLAY   GO

IT'S TIME FOR

GAME   EVENT   FANS

TOURNAMENT   TIME

CHAMPIONSHIP TEAM

PRACTICE

AEROBICS BIKE

CRAZEE OLYMPICS

FISHING FOOTBALL

FRISBEE GOLF
HOCKEY OLYMPICS
PING PONG RACE
RACKETBALL
SKATING SOCCER
SOFTBALL
SPECIAL OLYMPICS
SPORTS SURFING
SWIMMING TENNIS
VOLLEYBALL WARBALL

39

40

41

43

FOOD EVENTS

It is widely known that if you want to draw a crowd, serve food. These logos are designed to draw attention to a food event. Included are some generic words such as "All Church" or "Teen" that will help publicize a specific event.

Potluck

Refreshments

FOOD EVENT

Teen　Youth　All
Young Adult　Church

Pancake Feed
Chili Supper
Spaghetti Dinner
Pizza Party
Wienie Roast　Dessert
Potluck　Barbecue
Ice Cream　Picnic
Refreshments　Eats!

Burgers Popcorn Breakfast Buffet Food Bar Snacks Blast Bonanza Chow

PIZZA PARTY

54

TRIP INFO

Need to drum up some enthusiasm for a future expedition? These cartoons can be enlarged for use on posters and T-shirts or reduced to fit on a calendar or a newsletter. Included are some generic trip heads ("Road Trip," "Join Us") as well as some specific popular trips ("Bike Hike," "Ski Trip"). Add heads such as "What to Bring" and "Check List." Your trip information will be complete and attractively publicized.

AMUSEMENT PARK TRIP

Check List:

CAMP OUT

BIKE·A·THON

FLOAT TRIP

BEACH BOUND

CANOE TRIP

teen retreat

SKI TRIP

TRIP INFO:

WHEN:
WHERE:
HOW MUCH:
WHAT TO BRING:
WHAT _NOT_ TO BRING:

ZOO TRIP

WHAT TO BRING:

BE A GOOD HOUSEGUEST.

YOU'RE RIGHT, JACK. THEY DO HAVE BIGGER POTHOLES OUT HERE IN THE MISSION FIELD.

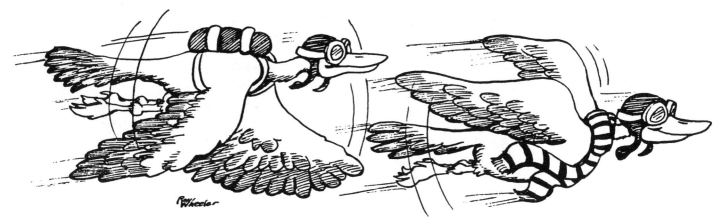

YOUTH FUNCTIONS

Rallies, Bible studies, retreats, service projects . . . all the important events that help the spiritual ministry of your group can be advertised with the items in this chapter. Many of the heads have been used by a specific denominational ministry, yet they are general enough to be effective for other youth ministries. Included are some generic words like "Youth" and "Teen" to use with words such as "Club" or "Missions."

CAMP
CLUB
DAY
GROUP
MEETING
MISSIONS
NIGHT
RALLY
TEEN
TIME

WEEK
YOUNG
YOUTH

FOOD DRIVE

CAR WASH

AAAAHHHHHHH

WEEKEND GETAWAY

Sunday School

"GETTING TO KNOW YOU" RALLY

PLANNING MEETING

ROUND-UP!

MUSIC NEWS

A music ministry can be promoted with the use of these cartoons, heads, and logos. The item can be used in such places as an ongoing newsletter column ("Music Review"), bulletin announcements ("Choir Practice"), posters ("Concert!"), or programs ("Sing along").

SPIRIT-FILLED FILLERS

Got a blank spot in your church newsletter that you need to fill? Does your brochure look too boring, busy, or hard to read? Do you need a gag cartoon or a comic strip to get a grin? Use one of these fillers to make your material sparkle.

GREAT MOMENTS IN CHURCH HISTORY:
THE UPPER ROOM HAS THEIR FIRST MISSIONS
CONFERENCE.

83

BE A HERO FOR GOD TODAY!

BE THE GREATEST

HOW WELL DO YOU EXPRESS LOVE?

THE POWER OF PRAYER

by Oppo Wheeler

THEY ARE WITHOUT EXCUSE

84

HOW DO YOU BUILD A TEMPLE?

GOD'S WINNING TEAM

THINGS ARE LOOKING UP

C.L.O.D.
CAMPUS LIFE OBSERVES DRINKING

I MET THE CHALLENGE!

FINDING
BODIES
IMMEDIATELY

HERE! HAVE A TRACT!

DON'T DISTRIBUTE YOUR TRACTS INDISCRIMINATELY.

FREE **HEART TRANSPLANT**

YEAH, OLE BERT THERE ... HE'S GOT AN EVANGELISM STYLE ALL HIS OWN.

WHAT'S YOUR **PROBLEM?**

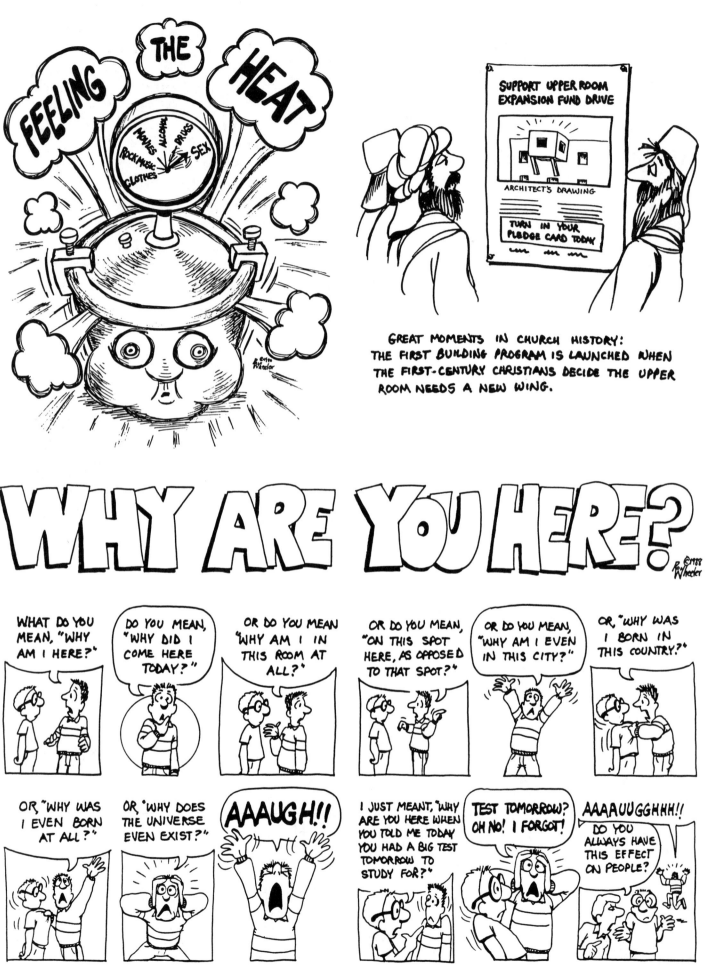

WHILE GRANDMA BABYSITS FOR LITTLE AMANDA, THE FEDERAL REGULATORS STAND BY TO MAKE SURE SHE DOESN'T OPEN THE "B" BOOK OR USE THE "G" OR "J" WORDS.

GREAT MOMENTS IN HISTORY:
"BECAUSE WE'VE ALWAYS DONE IT THIS WAY! THAT'S WHY!"
...IS SAID FOR THE FIRST TIME IN A CHURCH BOARD MEETING.

I'M TIRED OF THE OLD HYMNS! CAN'T WE DO SOMETHING CONTEMPORARY FOR A CHANGE?

MOST OF US ARE COMMITTED TO FURTHERING GOD'S KINGDOM, BUT WE'RE NOT QUITE SURE WHAT HAWKINS IS COMMITTED TO FURTHERING.

I TELL YOU, SALLY, YOU WOULDN'T BELIEVE HOW WIDESPREAD THESE PAGAN, SUPERSTITIOUS, OCCULTIC RELIGIONS ARE IN THE DEVELOPING NATIONS I'VE VISITED.

I'VE GOT NEWS FOR YOU, WILLIE.

OOOMMMMMM.

BOING   BOING   BOING

THEY'RE WIDE-SPREAD IN THE U.S., TOO.

SAY, HONEY, HAVEN'T WE MET BEFORE IN A PREVIOUS LIFE?

I KNOW I NEED TO COMMUNICATE WITH MY PARENTS BECAUSE DEEP DOWN THEY WANT TO KNOW WHAT I'M THINKING.

BUT IT'S KIND OF HARD TO BELIEVE THAT DAD'S REALLY INTERESTED IN LISTENING WHEN HIS NOSE IS ALWAYS BURIED IN THE NEWSPAPER.

WELL, HERE GOES! DAD, I WRECKED THE CAR TODAY.

WHAT?

WELL, WHATTYA KNOW. HE **IS** INTERESTED.

JUST FRIENDS!

WHAT IS A FRIEND? A FRIEND IS...

SOMEONE WHO NOTICES WHEN YOU HAVE YOUR BRACES OFF.

SOMEONE YOU CAN GET SILLY WITH.

SOMEONE WHO TELLS YOU YOUR SLIP IS SHOWING

SOMEONE WHO MOVES AWAY AND WHEN SHE COMES BACK IT DOESN'T SEEM AS IF SHE EVER LEFT.

SOMEONE WHO SHARES M&M'S WITH YOU.

GOD IS A FRIEND.

95

CALENDAR FIXIN'S

This chapter will give a lot of help. There are holiday ("Valentine's Day") and special occasion ("School's Out") cartoon logos. There is a one-month calendar ready for customizing with specific events for any year or month and several general usage words and numbers. Combine items to construct custom headers such as "Friday Night Live," or "Wednesday Morning Prayer Breakfast." These items can also be used to customize cartoon logos from previous chapters such as "Square Dance, October 23," or "Bible Study, Friday Night."

THANKSGIVING

CHRISTMAS CAROLING

Birthdays:

RUDOLPH'S RED-NOSED RALLY

JUNE

JULY

AUGUST

JANUARY

FEBRUARY

MARCH

APRIL

MAY

DECEMBER

NOVEMBER

OCTOBER

SEPTEMBER

YOUTH ACTIVITIES

BREAKFAST	PARTY
LUNCH	PRAISE
DINNER	NIGHT
SNACK	EVENING
BRUNCH	AFTERNOON
SUPPER	NOON
FELLOWSHIP	MORNING
BIBLE STUDY	WINTER
MEETING	SPRING
LIVE	SUMMER
PRAYER	FALL

MONDAY APRIL

TUESDAY MAY

WEDNESDAY JUNE

THURSDAY JULY

FRIDAY AUGUST

SATURDAY SEPTEMBER

SUNDAY OCTOBER

JANUARY NOVEMBER

FEBRUARY DECEMBER

MARCH MONTH

DAY YEAR 1991 2345678

Borders, Symbols, & Letters

Now you can let your creativity run wild. This chapter contains a variety of decorative symbols that can be reproduced several times and placed together to form borders, boxes, squares, and rectangles. There are also several easy to use cartoon-style balloons, banners, and boxes ready to promote your message. If you want to give that message a quality look, use the cartoon-lettering alphabets and numbers to make your message. Newsletter, stationery, and postcard mastheads are also included.

This is a good chapter to use in conjunction with other parts of the book. For example, you may want to print some fliers to promote a special trip. You could get the "It's Time for a" from the Sports Heads chapter, "Road Trip" and "When, Where, etc." from the Trip Info chapter, and the creative border from this chapter. You can also create your own posters and T-shirts to promote specific events. Simply use the alphabet from this chapter, along with a date from the Calendar Fixin's chapter, and add it to a special event drawing from the Party Promos chapter.

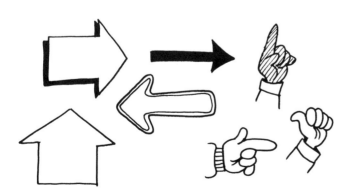

ABCDEFGHIJKLM
NOPQRSTUVWXYZ
abcdefghijklmn
opqrstuvwxyz?!
$";;¢1234567890

ANNOUNCING...

SPECIAL RECOGNITION!

IT'S TIME FOR A

ROAD TRIP

WHEN:
WHERE:
HOW MUCH:
WHAT TO BRING:
WHAT NOT TO BRING:

123

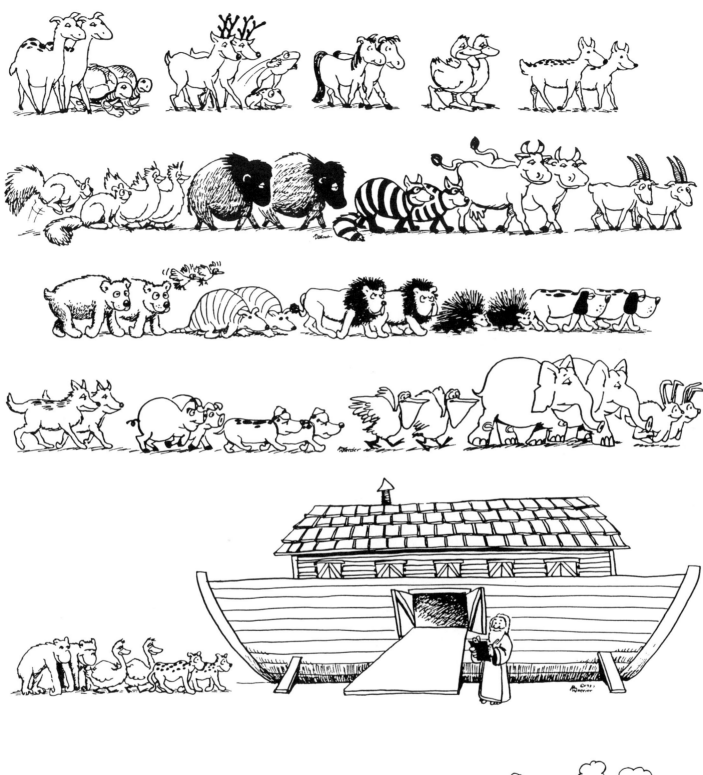

HERE'S WHAT'S HAPPENING IN SUNDAY SCHOOL

THE BIG LIE

SCRATCH PAD

ALL-PURPOSE SPOT CARTOONS

This chapter has a variety of fun cartoons that do not readily fit into any of the other sections. Use them as space fillers or to illustrate announcements in your newsletter.

GRUMBLE
GRUMBLE
GRUMBLE

137

IT'S

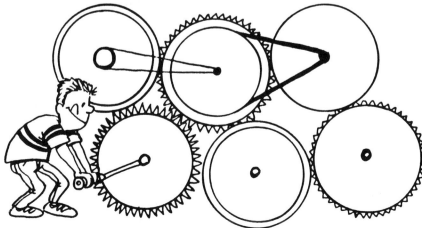

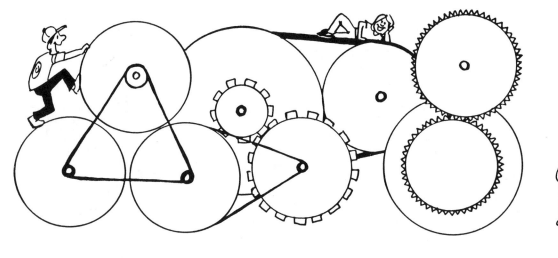

GACK!

BUT, CAROLYN, PAUL WROTE IN SECOND CORINTHIANS THAT WE SHOULD GREET ONE ANOTHER WITH A HOLY KISS.

144

HEY! WHO INVITED THE PRESCHOOLER?

NO SWIMMING

WILL I DO WELL IN MY NEW CLASS?

WILL MY TEACHER LIKE ME?

WILL I MAKE NEW FRIENDS?

A CHILD'S LOGIC

172

173

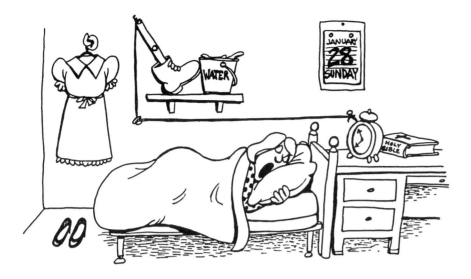

DON'T OVER-EMPHASIZE FINANCIAL NEEDS.

MAKE PERSONAL CONTACTS
WITH CHURCHES.

BE WILLING TO TALK TO
ANY GROUP

MOM, I NEED NEW JEANS!

MOM AT WORK

GIVE A CONCISE PRESENTATION
TO THE CHURCH

BE APPROPRIATELY DRESSED.

I'M OLD
ENOUGH
TO LOOK
AFTER
MYSELF!

WHY? WHY? WHY?

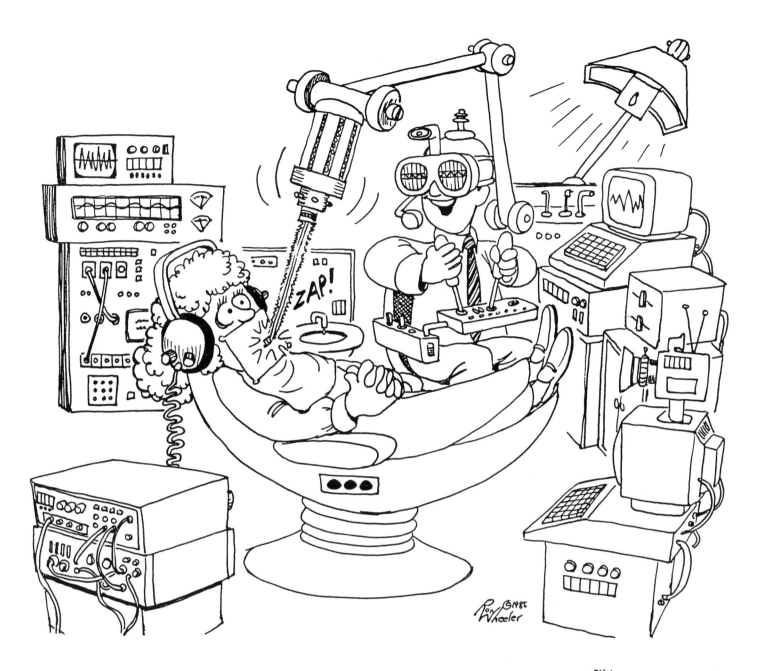

INDEX